Iron Hans

Matt Tavares
2008

To Hannah Nicole Robinson
and Kelsi Marie Robinson
— S. M.

For Rosemary
— M. T.

First edition 2007

Library of Congress Cataloging-in-Publication Data is available.
Library of Congress Catalog Card Number 2006047520

ISBN 978-0-7636-2160-5

10 9 8 7 6 5 4 3 2 1

Printed in Singapore

This book was typeset in Poliphilus MT.
The illustrations were done in watercolor and ink.

Candlewick Press
2067 Massachusetts Avenue
Cambridge, Massachusetts 02140

visit us at www.candlewick.com

IRON HANS

~ A Grimms' Fairy Tale ~

RETOLD BY STEPHEN MITCHELL

ILLUSTRATED BY MATT TAVARES

CANDLEWICK PRESS
CAMBRIDGE, MASSACHUSETTS

Once upon a time, there was a king who had a large forest near his palace, and in this forest there were all kinds of wild animals. One day he sent out a huntsman to shoot a deer, but the huntsman didn't come back. "Maybe he had an accident," the king said, so he sent out two more huntsmen to look for him, but they didn't come back either. On the third day, he sent for all his huntsmen and said, "Search the whole forest, and don't stop until you've found them." But none of the men came back, and of the many dogs they had taken with them, not one was ever seen again.

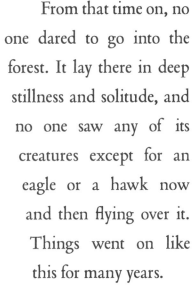

From that time on, no one dared to go into the forest. It lay there in deep stillness and solitude, and no one saw any of its creatures except for an eagle or a hawk now and then flying over it. Things went on like this for many years.

Then one day a huntsman appeared before the king, looking for a job, and offered to go into the dangerous forest. "It's not safe in there," the king said. "I'm afraid you'd do no better than the others, and you'd never come out again."

"Your Majesty," the huntsman said, "I will go in at my own risk. I don't know the meaning of fear."

So the huntsman took his dog and went into the forest. Soon the dog picked up the scent of some animal and began to follow it, but after it had run a few steps, it came to a deep pool and stopped. A large bare arm rose out of the water, grabbed the dog, and pulled it under.

The huntsman was appalled; it was his favorite dog, and he loved it very much. But he had a job to do, and he was determined to do it. "There is a huge, dangerous man at the bottom of the pool," he thought. "He can breathe underwater, and it will be hard to capture him by diving in. The only sensible way is to drain the pool." So he hurried off and brought back thirty men with buckets.

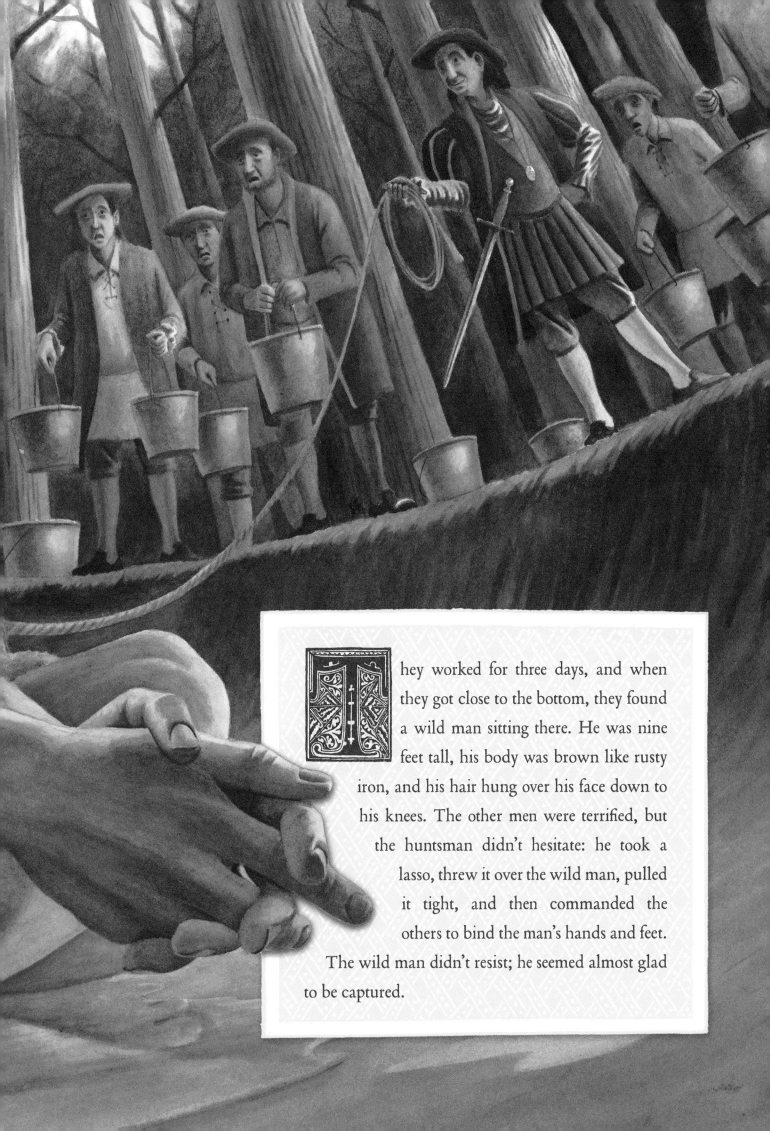

They worked for three days, and when they got close to the bottom, they found a wild man sitting there. He was nine feet tall, his body was brown like rusty iron, and his hair hung over his face down to his knees. The other men were terrified, but the huntsman didn't hesitate: he took a lasso, threw it over the wild man, pulled it tight, and then commanded the others to bind the man's hands and feet. The wild man didn't resist; he seemed almost glad to be captured.

They carried the wild man to the palace. Everyone was astonished. He was so huge and strange-looking that no one except the huntsman dared to get near him. The king commanded that he be locked in an iron cage in the palace courtyard. No one was allowed to open the door of the cage upon pain of death, and the key to it was entrusted to the queen herself. From that day on, it was safe to go into the forest.

The king had a son who was eight years old. One day, while he was playing in the courtyard, his golden ball rolled into the cage. The boy ran over and, frightened as he was, shouted into the cage, "Give me my ball!" This was the first time anyone had spoken to the wild man.

The wild man looked at the boy with surprise, then interest, then affection. Then he scowled and roared, "I won't give you your ball till you open the door for me."

"No," said the boy. "I won't do that; the king has forbidden it." And he ran away.

The next day, he came back and again asked for his ball. The wild man said, "Open my door."

"You know I can't do that," the boy said. "Besides, it would be dangerous to let you out. Everyone knows about the huntsmen and the dogs who never returned."

"I may be dangerous to others," said the wild man, "but not to you."

"Why did you kill those people?"

"Ah," sighed the wild man. "I'm under an evil spell, and I have to protect the golden spring. If anyone gets too close to it, I have to kill them. I don't like doing it, but I have no choice."

"Who put you under the spell?" asked the boy.

"I can't tell you now," the wild man said. "But trust me; I wasn't always like this."

The boy thought about this conversation all day. He grew more and more fascinated with the wild man, and less and less afraid of him.

n the third day, the king was out hunting, and the boy went back and said, "I really want to let you out, and I don't even care about getting my ball back. But I can't open the door, because I don't have the key." The wild man said, "It's under your mother's pillow. That's where you'll find it."

The boy was excited and terrified. Could he actually break his father's rules, betray his mother, and steal the key? By now the desire to let the wild man out of his cage was so strong that he knew he had to continue, even if he was caught in the act. He crept up to the queen's bedroom, took the key from beneath her pillow, and ran down the winding stairs as fast as he could. By the time he reached the cage, he could barely breathe.

He had a difficult time opening the door, and as he was pressing down on the key, he cut his finger. Finally the door opened, and the wild man stepped out, gave him the golden ball, and quickly began to walk away.

The boy yelled, "Wait! Please, wild man, don't go! Wait for me!" The wild man looked over his shoulder and turned back.

"What do you want?" he said.

"Take me with you, please!" said the boy.

"Why should I do that?"

"If you leave me here, they'll punish me. My father will be furious, and my mother too. I've never broken the rules before."

"Is that why you want to come with me?"

"I've never met anyone like you."

"Fine," said the wild man, and he leaned down, picked the boy up, put him on his shoulders, and with long strides hurried into the forest.

hen the king came home, he saw the empty cage and asked the queen what had happened. She didn't know, and she looked for the key, but it was gone. When they called for the prince, no one answered. The king sent men to look for him in the fields and near the pool where the wild man had been discovered, but they didn't find him. Finally the king guessed what had happened, and grief reigned in the royal court.

Once the wild man got back to the dark forest, he took the boy down from his shoulders and said, "You may never see your father and mother again, but I'll keep you with me, because you unlocked the cage, and I feel for you. If you do everything I tell you to, you'll be fine. I am very rich and powerful.

I am the richest man in the world." He made a bed of moss for the boy to sleep on, and that night the boy slept well and deeply.

In the morning, the wild man took him to a spring and said, "Look: this golden spring is as bright and clear as crystal. As long as it remains pure, I feel that there is hope for me and that someday the spell will be lifted. I want you to sit beside it and make sure that nothing falls into it, or it will be polluted. I'll come every evening to see if you've obeyed me."

The boy sat down at the edge of the spring and saw how now and then a golden fish or a golden snake appeared in the water. He was careful not to let anything fall in. After a while, though, the finger he'd cut started to ache again, and without thinking, he dipped it in the water. He quickly pulled it out again, but it had turned to gold, and try as he might to wash the gold off, he couldn't.

n the evening, the wild man came back, looked at the boy, and said, "What happened to the spring?"

"Nothing, nothing," the boy answered, holding his finger behind his back so that the wild man couldn't see it. He was so frightened and disappointed in himself that he had to lie.

But the wild man knew. "You dipped your finger in the spring," he said. "Didn't I tell you that nothing must enter the spring or it will be polluted? I'll let it pass this time, but make sure it doesn't happen again."

Early the next morning, the boy was sitting by the spring, keeping watch. His finger ached again, he touched his head, and then, unluckily, one of his hairs fell into the spring and turned gold.

The moment the wild man arrived, he knew what had happened. "You've let a hair fall into the spring," he said. "I'll overlook it once more, but if this happens again, the spring will be polluted and you'll have to leave."

On the third day, the boy was sitting beside the spring, and however much his finger hurt him, he didn't move it. But the time passed slowly, and he looked down at the reflection of his face. And as he bent closer and closer, trying to look himself straight in the eyes, his long hair fell from his shoulders into the water. He straightened up quickly, but his hair had already turned to gold and shone like a sun. You can imagine how upset and frightened the boy was. He took his handkerchief and tied it around his head, so that the man wouldn't see his hair.

But the moment the wild man arrived, he knew everything and said, "Take off the handkerchief." The golden hair came streaming down, and however much the boy apologized, it was of no use. "You can't stay here any longer. Go out into the world. You'll learn what it is to be poor. But since you have a good heart and I wish you well, I'll grant you one favor: if you're ever in trouble, come to the forest and shout, 'Iron Hans!' and I'll come and help you. My power is great, greater than you can imagine, and I am the richest man in the world."

The boy felt crushed. It had been such a simple task to watch over the golden spring, and he had failed. He didn't know why he wanted to stay with Iron Hans, but he longed to, more than anything. Was it because of the man's wildness or his gentleness?

It was obvious, though, that the boy had to leave now, and this saddened him, though it was a comfort to know he could always call on Iron Hans if he got into trouble.

As the boy left the forest, he considered returning home, but the thought of his old life, with its rules and routines, made him even sadder. Ever since he had met Iron Hans, he felt changed, and he knew he could never go back. He also knew that part of this new test was learning how to be poor and powerless. He would have to keep his identity hidden and let no one guess that he was a prince.

He traveled over beaten and unbeaten paths until at last he came to a great city in another kingdom. When he looked for work there, he couldn't find any; since he had always been a prince, he had never learned anything that would help him earn his living. Finally he went to the palace and asked if they would give him a job. The courtiers didn't know what use they could make of him, but they liked him and let him stay. Eventually the cook put him to work carrying wood and water and sweeping up ashes.

nce, when no one else was available, the cook told him to bring the trays of food to the royal table, and the boy kept his hat on since he didn't want anyone to notice his golden hair. It was so radiant that people would immediately know that he wasn't as ordinary as he seemed.

When the king saw him with his hat on, he said, "What an extraordinarily rude young fellow you are! Didn't anyone ever teach you manners? Even a five-year-old knows that when you come to the royal table, you must take off your hat."

"Oh, but I can't do that, Your Majesty," the boy answered. "I have ugly scales all over my head. You'd be disgusted if you saw them."

The king summoned the cook. "How can you let a boy like that work for you?" he shouted. "Fire him immediately."

But the cook felt for the boy, and instead of firing him, he traded him for the gardener's assistant.

Now the boy had to work in the garden, planting and watering and hoeing and digging, even in wind and bad weather. One day, in the summer, when he was working alone in the garden, it was so hot that he took off his hat to cool his head in the breeze. His hair was so bright that it flashed into the bedroom of the king's daughter, and she jumped up to see what the light was. She caught sight of the boy and called to him, "Boy, go get me a bunch of flowers!" He quickly put on his hat, picked a bunch of wildflowers, and tied a string around them. As he was walking up the stairs, he passed the gardener, who said, "How can you bring the princess such common flowers? Quick, go out and pick another bunch, and gather only the rarest and most beautiful ones."

"Oh, no," said the boy. "Wildflowers are more fragrant, and she'll like them better." He had no doubt that this was true.

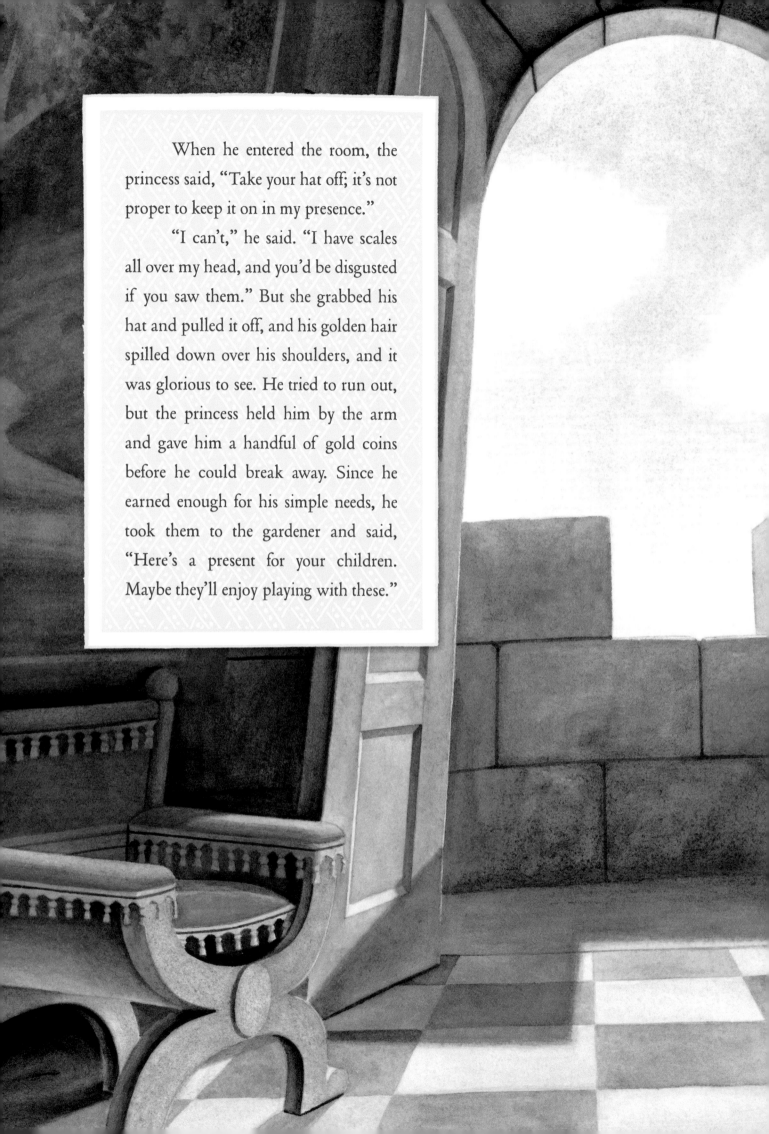

When he entered the room, the princess said, "Take your hat off; it's not proper to keep it on in my presence."

"I can't," he said. "I have scales all over my head, and you'd be disgusted if you saw them." But she grabbed his hat and pulled it off, and his golden hair spilled down over his shoulders, and it was glorious to see. He tried to run out, but the princess held him by the arm and gave him a handful of gold coins before he could break away. Since he earned enough for his simple needs, he took them to the gardener and said, "Here's a present for your children. Maybe they'll enjoy playing with these."

ome time later, the country was overrun by war. The king called up his troops, but he didn't know whether they could defeat the enemy, who was very powerful and had a large army.

The prince said, "I'm grown up now, and I want to go to war too. Just give me a horse."

The other servants laughed and said, "We'll leave one in the stable for you." When they'd left, he went to the stable. The horse they'd left was lame in one leg, and it limped, *clumpetty-clip, clumpetty-clip.* But he mounted it anyway and rode off to the dark forest.

When he came to the edge of the forest, he shouted "Iron Hans!" three times, so loudly that his voice echoed through the trees. Right away the wild man appeared and said, "What do you want?"

"I want a strong horse, because I'm going to the war."

"That's what you'll have," said Iron Hans, "and even more than you asked for." Then he went back into the forest, and in a short time a groom came out, leading a powerful stallion that snorted and was so eager to run that it could hardly be reined back. Behind them rode a large troop of warriors in iron armor, and their swords flashed in the sunlight. The prince gave his three-legged nag to the groom, mounted the powerful stallion, and rode off at the head of the troop.

When he reached the battle-field, he saw that many of the king's men had been killed, and it was clear that the rest would soon have to surrender. The prince galloped up with his iron warriors, fell on the enemy like a thunderstorm, and struck down everyone who opposed him. The enemy troops ran away, but the prince rode after them and pursued them until not a single man was left. All during the battle, he was filled with a feeling of great calm and satisfaction. Everything he did was effortless. His sword seemed as light as a twig, and he felt that nothing could touch him. It was as if he were in a sweet dream.

fter the battle was over, instead of returning to the king, he led his warriors back to the forest and shouted for Iron Hans.

"What do you want?" asked the wild man.

"Take back your stallion and your soldiers, and give me my three-legged nag." Then he rode the lame horse back home.

When the king returned to the palace, his daughter came to congratulate him. "Yes, it was a great victory," the king said, "but the victory wasn't mine. The battle was won by a knight who came with a troop of iron warriors."

"Who was this knight?" the princess asked.

"I have no idea," the king said. "Whoever he was, he galloped off after the enemy, and I never saw him again."

"Isn't there some way we can send for him?" the princess said.

"There is," said the king. "I'm going to proclaim a great festival: it will last for three days, and you'll throw out a golden apple. I'll bet that the unknown knight will appear."

hen the festival was announced, the prince went out to the forest and shouted for Iron Hans.

"What do you want?" he said.

"I want to catch the princess's golden apple."

"It will be as you wish," said Iron Hans. "You'll also have a suit of red armor and ride a strong chestnut horse."

✳

When the day came, the prince came galloping up and took his place among the knights. No one recognized him. The princess stepped forward and threw a golden apple to the knights, and the prince caught it. As soon as he had it in his hand, he galloped away.

 n the second day, Iron Hans equipped him in armor and gave him a white horse. Again he caught the apple, and again he galloped off with it. The king was furious and said, "That's absolutely forbidden. Any knight who catches the apple must appear before me and tell me his name." He gave orders to his men that if the knight rode off again, they should gallop after him, and if he didn't come back willingly, they were to strike him down with their swords.

On the third day, Iron Hans gave the prince black armor and a black horse, and again he caught the apple. But as he was galloping off, the king's men rode after him, and one of them came near enough to wound the prince's leg with the tip of his sword. The prince escaped, but his horse reared so abruptly that his helmet fell off, and everyone could see his golden hair. They rode back and told the king everything that had happened.

he next day, the princess asked the gardener about his assistant. "He's working in the garden," the gardener said. "What a strange fellow he is! He went to the festival and didn't come back till yesterday evening, and he showed my children three golden apples he'd won."

The king sent for him, and when he came in, he was wearing his hat. But the princess went up to him and took it off, and his golden hair spilled down over his shoulders, and it was so beautiful that everyone was amazed. "Were you the knight who came to the festival, each day in a different color, and caught the three golden apples?" the king asked.

"Yes," said the prince, "and here they are." He took the apples out of his pocket and handed them to the king.

Since the king had asked him directly, the time had come to reveal his identity. The prince felt that he had passed all the tests that life, or Iron Hans, had given him. He had learned how to be poor and unknown and happy. He had learned how to ask for what he wanted. And he had learned how to be fearless and wild. "If you want further proof," he told the king, "look at the wound your men gave me when they were chasing me. And I must also tell you that I am the knight who helped you win the battle."

"If you can do such deeds, you are no gardener's assistant. Tell me, who are you?"

"My father is a king, and I was born into wealth and privilege," said the prince. "But I have also been poor, and poverty has taught me well."

"I see that I'm much indebted to you," said the king. "Is there anything I can do for you?"

"Yes, there is," he answered. "You can let me marry your daughter."

"Well!" said the girl, laughing. "He certainly isn't shy! But I always suspected that he wasn't really a gardener's assistant." Then she went over and kissed him.

he prince's father and mother were invited to the wedding, and they were overjoyed; they had given up hope of ever seeing their dear son again. When all the guests were seated at the marriage table, the music suddenly stopped, the doors opened, and a stately king came in with a great number of attendants. He walked up to the prince, embraced him, and said, "I am Iron Hans. By becoming a fine, modest, brave young man, you have passed the test, and you have set me free from the evil spell that turned me from an arrogant king into a wild man. I am as proud of you as your own father and mother could be. And to show my gratitude, I am leaving my whole kingdom to you and your beautiful bride."

The prince was deeply touched and
felt a tear drop from his eye. He called for the
largest chair in the palace, and when Iron
Hans sat down in it, the music began again.